Dear Parents and Educators,

Welcome to Penguin Young Readers! As parents and educators, you know that each child develops at his or her own pace—in terms of speech, critical thinking, and, of course, reading. Penguin Young Readers recognizes this fact. As a result, each Penguin Young Readers book is assigned a traditional easy-to-read level (1–4) as well as a Guided Reading Level (A–P). Both of these systems will help you choose the right book for your child. Please refer to the back of each book for specific leveling information. Penguin Young Readers features esteemed authors and illustrators, stories about favorite characters, fascinating nonfiction, and more!

The Barker Twins™: Hide-and-Seek All Week

LEVEL 2

GUIDED READING LEVEL **I**

This book is perfect for a **Progressing Reader** who:
- can figure out unknown words by using picture and context clues;
- can recognize beginning, middle, and ending sounds;
- can make and confirm predictions about what will happen in the text; and
- can distinguish between fiction and nonfiction.

Here are some **activities** you can do during and after reading this book:
- Problems: The problem in this story is that the kids can't decide on the rules for the game, even after trying to do so for the whole week of school! On a separate piece of paper, write down the days of the week. Below each day, write down the problem the kids face.
- Make Predictions: At the end of the story, Moffie says she will make rules for making the rules and bring them in on Monday. What do you think will happen when the kids get to school on Monday?

Remember, sharing the love of reading with a child is the best gift you can give!

—Bonnie Bader, EdM
  Penguin Young Readers program

*Penguin Young Readers are leveled by independent reviewers applying the standards developed by Irene Fountas and Gay Su Pinnell in *Matching Books to Readers: Using Leveled Books in Guided Reading*, Heinemann, 1999.

For Sherry Litwack, who rivals
Moffie and Sally in the "Fashion World,"
Fraser and Alexander, and, of course, Mario.

Jennifer Smith-Stead, Literacy Consultant

Penguin Young Readers
Published by the Penguin Group
Penguin Group (USA) Inc., 375 Hudson Street, New York, New York 10014, USA
Penguin Group (Canada), 90 Eglinton Avenue East, Suite 700, Toronto, Ontario M4P 2Y3, Canada
(a division of Pearson Penguin Canada Inc.)
Penguin Books Ltd., 80 Strand, London WC2R 0RL, England
Penguin Group Ireland, 25 St. Stephen's Green, Dublin 2, Ireland (a division of Penguin Books Ltd.)
Penguin Group (Australia), 250 Camberwell Road, Camberwell, Victoria 3124, Australia
(a division of Pearson Australia Group Pty. Ltd.)
Penguin Books India Pvt. Ltd., 11 Community Centre, Panchsheel Park, New Delhi—110 017, India
Penguin Group (NZ), 67 Apollo Drive, Rosedale, Auckland 0632, New Zealand
(a division of Pearson New Zealand Ltd.)
Penguin Books (South Africa) (Pty.) Ltd., 24 Sturdee Avenue,
Rosebank, Johannesburg 2196, South Africa

Penguin Books Ltd., Registered Offices: 80 Strand, London WC2R 0RL, England

Library of Congress Control Number: 2001055627

ISBN 978-0-448-42545-0   10 9 8 7 6 5 4 3 2

PENGUIN YOUNG READERS

Level

2

PROGRESSING READER

⭐ THE BARKER TWINS™

HIDE-AND-SEEK ALL WEEK

by Tomie dePaola

Penguin Young Readers
An Imprint of Penguin Group (USA) Inc.

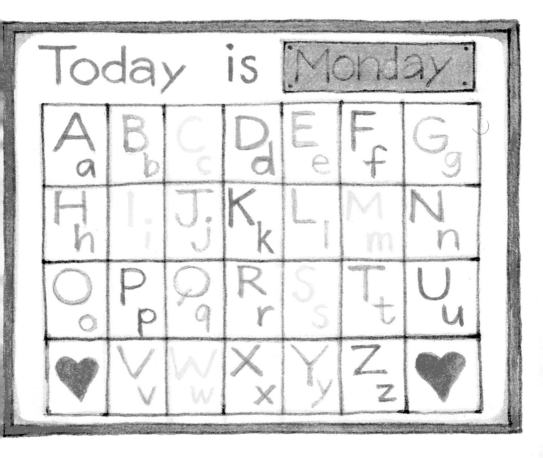

All the kids in kindergarten
were writing their names.
Moffie wrote M-O-F-F-A-T.
Morgie wrote M-O-R-G-A-N.
"Good job!" Ms. Shepherd
told the twins.

RING!

"There is the bell for recess,"

Ms. Shepherd said.

"Class, you have worked hard.

Now it is time to play."

BOBB

Everyone ran out

to the playground.

"Let's play Hide-and-Seek,"

Morgie said to Billy.

Moffie and Sally wanted to play.

"I will be IT," Moffie said.

But Morgie shook his head.

"We have to pick who will be IT."

Morgie wanted to toss a coin.

Sally wanted

to do One Potato, Two Potato.

Billy wanted to go by the ABCs

because "Billy" began with a B.

"I have the most gold stars,"

Moffie said.

"So I should be IT!"

"I have gold stars, too," Sally said.

"Let's ask Ms. Shepherd,"

Billy said.

 **RING!**

Recess was over.

"We will have to wait

until tomorrow,"

Morgie said.

There was the bell for recess.

"Class, put away your crayons

and your maps," Ms. Shepherd said.

The four friends got ready

to play Hide-and-Seek.

"We can decide who is IT later,"

Moffie said.

"Now we need rules about hiding."

"I will make a map," Sally said.

"The swings are

out-of-bounds," Billy said.

"The tubes are too easy,"

Moffie said.

"The tree is too tall," Sally said.

"I don't like to climb."

Recess was over.

"We will have to wait

until tomorrow," Billy said.

"Good," Ms. Shepherd said.

"Now everyone can count to ten."

There was the bell for recess.

The four friends met by the slide.

"We forgot counting rules,"

Moffie said.

"I can count to twenty,"

Sally said.

"I can only count to ten,"

Morgie said.

"You can count to ten *two* times,"

Billy said.

"Ten and ten make twenty."

"Okay!" Morgie said.

"But you are not IT," Moffie said.

"And we still don't have a map."

"We will have to wait
until tomorrow," Sally said.

The next day it was raining.

"We must stay inside today,"

Ms. Shepherd said.

They went to the gym for recess.

"Well," Moffie said, "we can't play

Hide-and-Seek in here!"

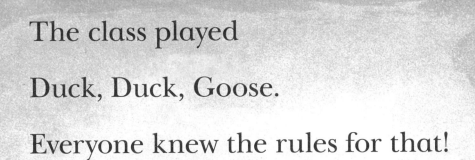

The class played

Duck, Duck, Goose.

Everyone knew the rules for that!

"Hand in hand, Hansel and Gretel

ran all the way home,"

Ms. Shepherd read.

"The end."

Ms. Shepherd closed the book.

 RING!

It was recess.

"We can't play Hide-and-Seek yet.

We need to pick home base,"

Moffie said.

"Home can be the tree,"

Morgie said.

"I don't like the tree," Sally said.

"Home can be the school wall."

"No," Billy said.

"Home can be the slide."

No one could decide.

"Let's forget about

Hide-and-Seek," Morgie said.

"Let's play Steal the Bacon.

We can get some more

kids to play."

"First we have to make the rules,"
Billy said.

Everybody nodded.

"But this time we need *rules*
for making the rules,"
Sally said.

"I will do that," Moffie said.

"I will have them ready

for Monday!"